Grandma and Grandpa Cruise
Alaska's Inside Passage

by
Bernd and Susan Richter

Published by
Alaska Children's Books, Wasilla, Alaska, USA

Dedicated to our sister and brothers

Ingo Richter, Zoltan Koi, Regina Neely,
Miklos Koi, and Julian Koi.

Acknowledgement:
We owe special thanks to Linda Thurston for her
editing effort and suggestions.

More children's books and games by Bernd and Susan Richter, Alaska Children's Books:

* *A Bus Ride Into Denali (folding book)*
* *Alaska Animals - Where Do They Go At 40 Below?*
* *Alaskan Toys - For Girls and Boys (folding book)*
* *Cruising Alaska's Inside Passage*
* *Discover Alaska's Denali Park*
* *Do Alaskans Live in Igloos?*
* *Good Morning Alaska - Good Morning Little Bear (bb)*
* *Goodnight Alaska - Goodnight Little Bear (board book)*
* *Grandma and Grandpa Cruise Alaska's Inside Passage*
* *Grandma and Grandpa Love Their RV*
* *Grandma and Grandpa Ride the Alaska Train*
* *Grandma and Grandpa Visit Denali National Park*
* *How Alaska Got its Flag (with Alaska flag song CD)*
* *How Animal Moms Love Their Babies (board book)*
* *Listen to Alaska's Animals (sound book)*
* *Listen to the Alaska Train (sound book)*
* *My Alaska Animals - Can You Name Them? (folding b.)*
* *Peek-A-Boo Alaska (Lift-the-Flap board book)*

* *She's My Mommy Too!*
* *The Little Bear Who Didn't want to Hibernate*
* *The Twelve Days of Christmas in Alaska*
* *There Was a Little Bear (board book)*
* *There Was a Little Porcupine (board book)*
* *Touch and Feel Alaska's Animals (board book)*
* *Traveling Alaska*
* *Uncover Alaska's Wonders (Lift-the-Flap book)*
* *When Grandma and Grandpa Cruised Through Alaska (board b.)*
* *When Grandma and Grandpa Rode the White Pass Train (board b.)*
* *When Grandma and Grandpa Rode the Alaska Train (board b.)*
* *When Grandma and Grandpa Visited Alaska (board book)*
* *When Grandma and Grandpa visited Denali N. P. (board b.)*
* *When Grandma visited Alaska*
* *When I Cruised Through Alaska (board book)*
    * *Old Maid - Alaska Style (card game)*
    * *Alaska Animal Block Puzzle (12-block puzzle)*
    * *Alaska Animal ABC Puzzle Train (7-foot jigsaw puzzle)*

Look at these books and games by visiting our website **www.alaskachildrensbooks.com**

Dear ....

    With this picture book Grandma and Grandpa want to share with you their great cruise experience in Alaska.

    Why Alaska and why a cruise, you ask?

    Well, for one, Alaska has more wilderness areas than any other state in the United States. Here, people still live with bears, moose, caribou, and wolves in their backyards. Second, Alaska has a great history full of adventure and gold rushes. And the best and most comfortable way to see and experience all of this is by cruise ship.

    So here's how Grandma and Grandpa spent their vacation cruise traveling the Inside Passage of Alaska and some of the things they saw along the way. Enjoy!

Love, ...

Here's a map showing you where Alaska is. As you can easily see, Alaska is by far the largest of the 50 U.S. states.

This cruise will take Grandma and Grandpa to the southeastern part of Alaska, which is formed by a narrow strip of coastal land and by thousands of islands. These islands serve as a protective barrier from the Pacific Ocean for ships that navigate these waters. This is why this route is known as the 'Inside Passage' as opposed to an 'outside' passage along the open ocean.

Most cruise ships that sail the Inside Passage depart from Vancouver, British Columbia, in Canada, or from Seward or Whittier, Alaska, but some ships also sail from Seattle, Washington, or from San Francisco, California. Ask Grandma and Grandpa which city they departed from.

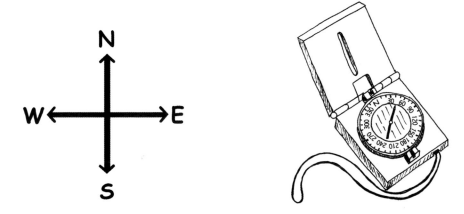

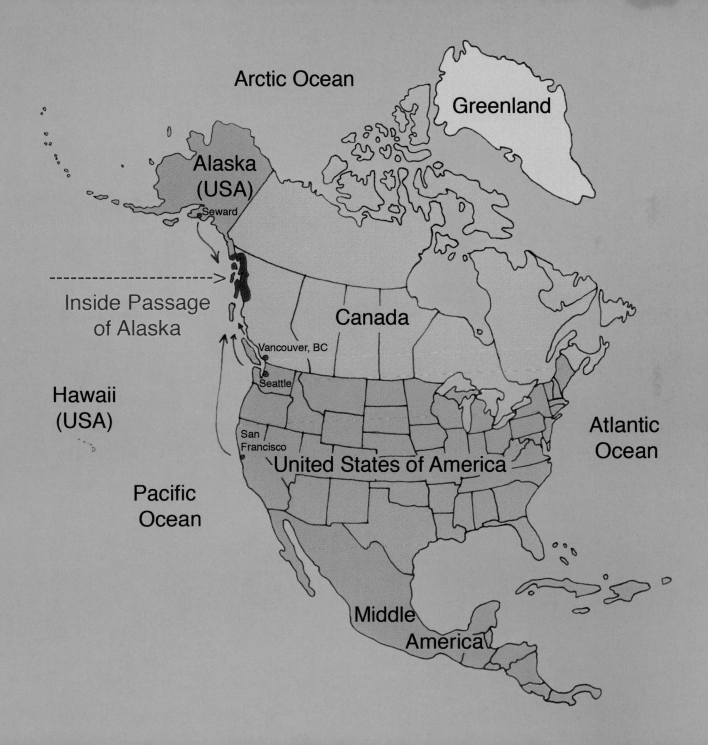

Here's the cruise ship at the city dock waiting for its passengers to get on. It is gorgeous, isn't it? And look how BIG it is! It is 16 stories high and longer than two football fields!

How many people do you think this ship holds? One hundred, perhaps? Or possibly one thousand? The captain tells Grandma and Grandpa that it accommodates 2,500 passengers and another 1,000 crewmembers. That's more people than in a small town! How can so many people live on a single ship? Where will Grandma and Grandpa find a place to sleep? Where will they shop and eat? Where can they go to have some fun?

Come on, let's get on board and find out.

Wow, the inside is beautiful! Everything sparkles and shines in the atrium, the main room that is several stories high and serves as a central meeting point for all the people on board.

The ship is so big Grandma and Grandpa need a map at first to find their way around. Actually, Grandpa thinks he doesn't need a map, but Grandma insisted on picking one up. The map is almost like a city map only it shows a cross section of all decks in the ship instead of streets and houses. There are cabins on almost every deck. And look, some decks have shops, movie theaters, swimming pools, even a basketball court and, what fun, game rooms for the children. It really is like a floating city!

The decks are connected by several elevators. Grandma and Grandpa locate the one closest and check out their room.

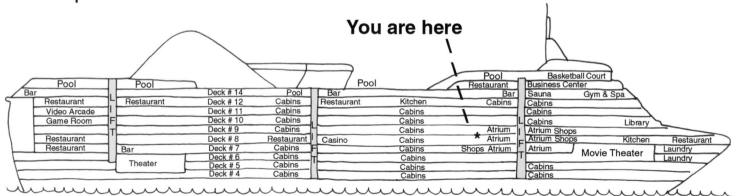

"Ah, our home away from home," Grandpa says to Grandma as they walk into their beautiful cabin, as a room is usually called on a ship. Most cabins aren't very big, but they have all the amenities Grandma and Grandpa need to be very comfortable, that is, one or two beds, a TV, a refrigerator, a telephone, a small bathroom with shower and, look, even a balcony. With their very own balcony Grandma and Grandpa won't miss any of the beautiful scenery on their Alaska cruise. Ask Grandma and Grandpa if their cabin looked like this.

Whoa, what is this? Is the ship moving? Yes, it is! Grandma and Grandpa quickly go to the viewing deck to watch the city disappear.

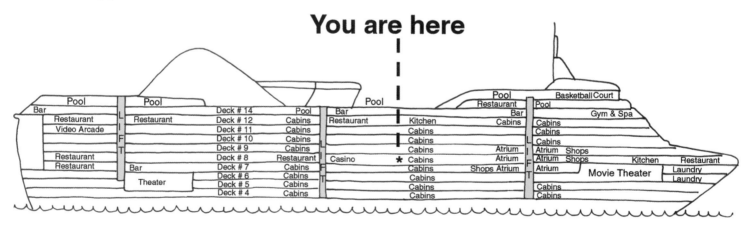

8

Grandma and Grandpa made it just in time to wave the city good-bye. The cruise has officially started. Grandma and Grandpa wonder what Alaska will be like? They read in their guide book that winters there last for up to seven months and they saw pictures of mountains that were covered with snow and ice even in the summer. And they read that in some areas the ground is frozen all year long. Brr, that must be cold! Alaskans probably don't walk barefoot a lot, do you think? Grandma and Grandpa hope they brought enough warm clothing. Grandma wanted to, but Grandpa wanted to travel light, of course!

You are here

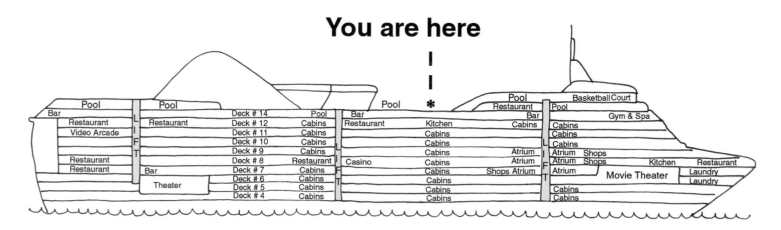

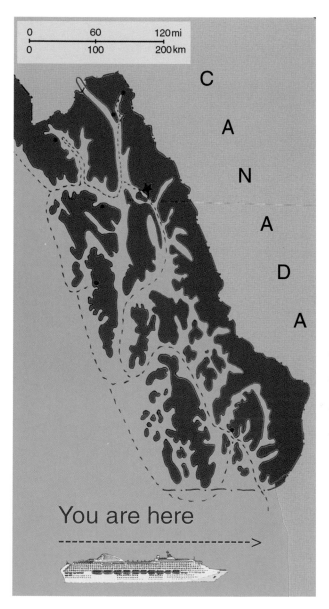

0 60 120mi
0 100 200km

C
A
N
A
D
A

You are here

- ->

The scenery certainly changed quickly, didn't it? Instead of houses, cars, and asphalt, Grandma and Grandpa now enjoy the sight of millions of trees, an occasional fishing boat, and water - lots and lots of water. It's so relaxing to watch the waves and the world go by. But Grandma and Grandpa also keep an eye out for whales and sea otters, which sometimes swim right by the ship. Ask Grandma and Grandpa if they saw any sea wildlife.

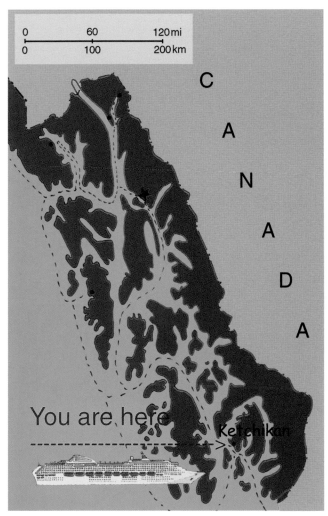

C
A
N
A
D
A

You are here

Ketchikan

After sailing all day and all night Grandma and Grandpa arrive at their southernmost stop in Alaska - Ketchikan. It takes a hearty soul to live in Ketchikan because this is not a sunny place. Some people call Ketchikan the 'rain capital' of Alaska because, on average, it rains here two out of three days. That makes for a lot of rained-out baseball practices! But on a nice day like today, Ketchikan is very pretty. Just look at this historic boardwalk area that is built on wooden pilings. Have you ever seen a creek where a street should be? Can you imagine having a creek under your house?

If you thought the houses over the creek were strange, then you have to have a look at this one with the totem poles!

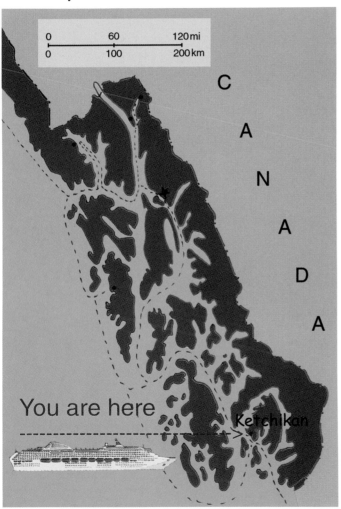

0 60 120 mi
0 100 200 km

C
A
N
A
D
A

You are here

Ketchikan

Ketchikan has the largest collection of totem poles in the world and Grandma and Grandpa are anxious to learn more about them. Totem poles were and are being made by Ketchikan's Tlingit Indian people. The beautiful wood-carvings show the symbols of things that are important to the Indian people, such as eagles, ravens, bears, whales, fish, and, of course, human faces. All those symbols combine to tell stories just like this book does. Can you identify some of these symbols?

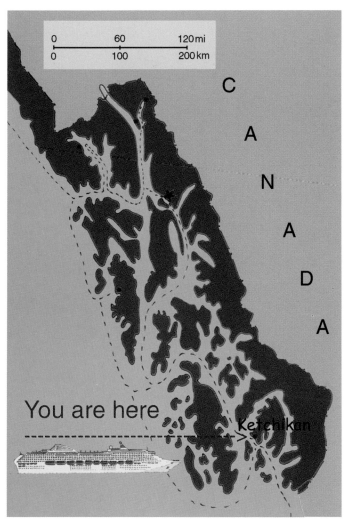

Some of the Alaska Natives who live in this area have come in their traditional regalia to dance for us. Just look how beautiful those robes are. Alaska Natives have lived in this part of Alaska for thousands of years before the white man arrived some 200 years ago. Nowadays, Alaska Natives live and dress like you and me. But in the old days, they certainly dressed differently, didn't they?

What an exciting day this was! Adventure makes Grandma and Grandpa hungry, which is why they are now looking forward to a great dinner at one of the restaurants on board of the cruise ship. Every night the chefs cook dishes from different countries in the world.

Tonight is Italian night. Grandma and Grandpa read the menu.
* Pappardelle al Sugo di Pollo,
* Pesce Spada alla Griglia,
They look at each other with big eyes before the waiter turns over the menu to show the English translation. That's better!
* Homemade egg noodles simmered with tender braised chicken and roasted red and yellow peppers in a rich demi-glace and sage sauce,
* Grilled swordfish with herb butter, broccoli and steamed potatoes,
* Shrimp flambéed in brandy with pearl rice and a fiery tomato sauce, and so much more.

That's a difficult choice, isn't it? Of course, there's also pizza and spaghetti with meatballs, if you'd like.

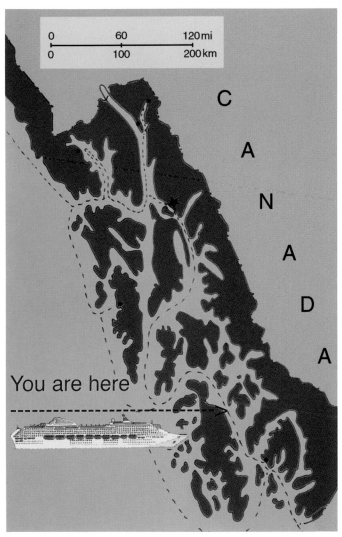

0   60   120 mi
0   100   200 km

C
A
N
A
D
A

You are here

After a good night's sleep Grandma and Grandpa are ready for a new day of adventure. There's not enough time to stop at every village, so the ship is sailing past this one. Almost everybody who makes his home on the Inside Passage lives within walking distance to the water's edge. So it's no surprise that most folks here own a boat and that many families make a living by fishing. Do you like to eat fish? Grandma and Grandpa tried some salmon and halibut during their cruise and found it d e l i c i o u s! You should try some when you get the chance.

Today's port of call is Juneau, the capital of Alaska. This is the site of the first big gold rush in Alaska more than 100 years ago. Like so many villages and cities on the Inside Passage, Juneau

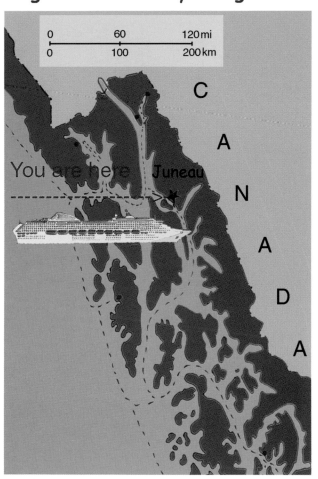

is squeezed onto a narrow strip of land between the water and the mountains. These steep mountains reach all the way to the coast in many places, which is why there aren't any roads connecting most of the towns and villages that we will see on our cruise. In other words, these towns have no road connections to the rest of the world.

There are streets in this city, of course. After all, about 30,000 people live in Juneau. But if they want to go somewhere out of town, they have to do so by boat or airplane.

If you thought it's strange that no roads lead to Juneau, then take a look at this! Just outside the city center is a huge **glacier**!

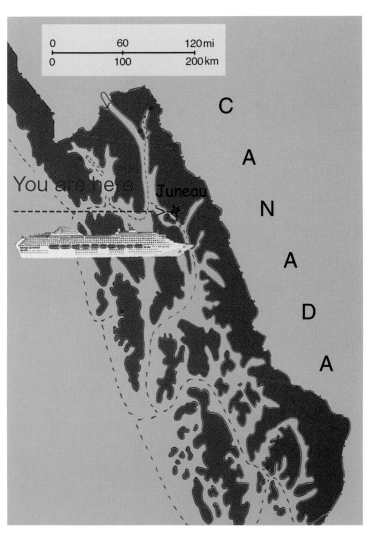

What is a glacier you want to know? And how did it get there? Well, a glacier is a massive river of ice that formed high up in the mountains where it is too cold for the snow to melt. When the ice got too heavy it slowly moved downhill until it ended up right here in this valley.

Most people take the bus to see this glacier. Others are more adventurous and hire a **helicopter**! What a thrill that must be! Have you ever been in a helicopter? If not, would you like to one day? Ask Grandma and Grandpa if they visited the glacier and how they got there.

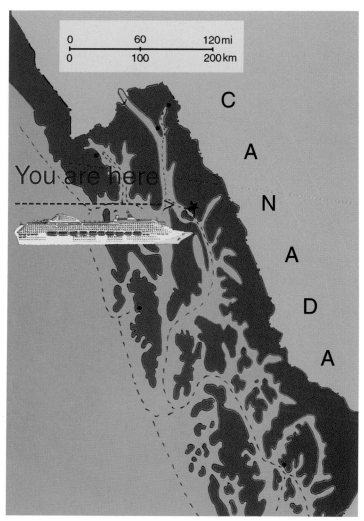

You are here

W hat an experience that was to see a glacier close up! But there's not only adventure on land. There's also excitement on the ship. Alaska is famous for its wild animals, both on land and in the water. Sometimes animals come so close to the ship that they can be seen from the viewing decks or the balconies. Looks like today is a great day for animal viewing. Can you see:
- the fierce grizzly bear,
- the killer whale,
- the cute sea otters,
- the funny-looking puffins,
- and the lazy seals?
Ask Grandma and Grandpa which animals they saw on their cruise.

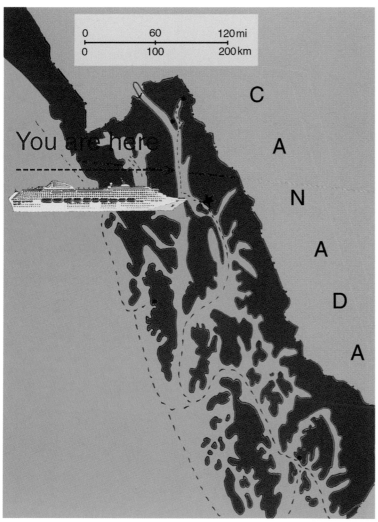

You are here

0   60   120 mi
0   100   200 km

C
A
N
A
D
A

*C*ruise ships usually stay at ports of call for most of the day to allow for sight-seeing on land. Then the ship sails through the night to its next destination. To find his way at night, the captain uses modern high-tech radar, sonar, radio signals, and computers. The bright lights of buoys and lighthouses help him identify landmarks on maps and warn him of rocks and shallow water that could be dangerous to the ship. That way Grandma and Grandpa sleep safely at night.

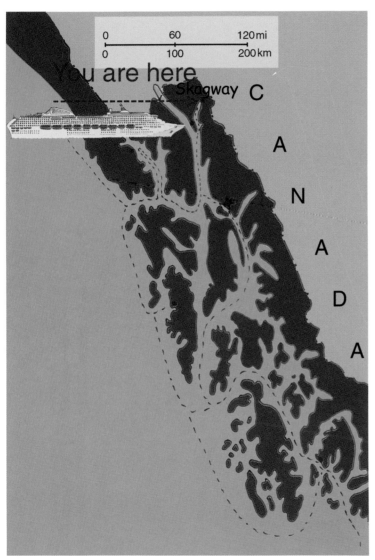

You are here

Skagway

C

A

N

A

D

A

| 0 | 60 | 120mi |
| 0 | 100 | 200km |

While Grandma and Grandpa were asleep, the ship docked at their next port of call, Skagway, and the crew prepared breakfast for an early start of another fun-filled day. Have you ever been on a train? There are two trains waiting for Grandma and Grandpa right here at the ship's dock. So let's go for a ride! The trains take the same route across the mountains that gold miners took over a hundred years ago on their way to mining claims during the Klondike Gold Rush. Should be a fun ride, don't you think?

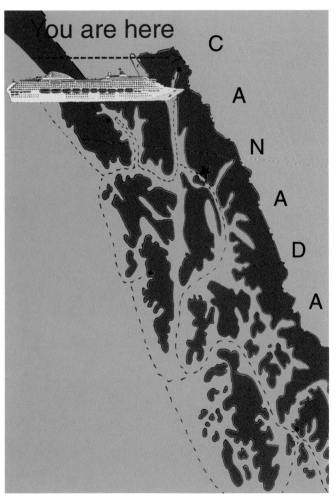

You are here

C
A
N
A
D
A

Grandma and Grandpa are having a blast! What a thrill it is to ride the train along steep mountainsides, through dark tunnels, and over old wooden bridges. It's almost like a roller coaster, only much, much slower.

When the gold rush started in 1897 the train didn't exist yet, and thousands of miners had to walk up the mountains along treacherous trails. Can you imagine how glad the miners were once the railroad started running?

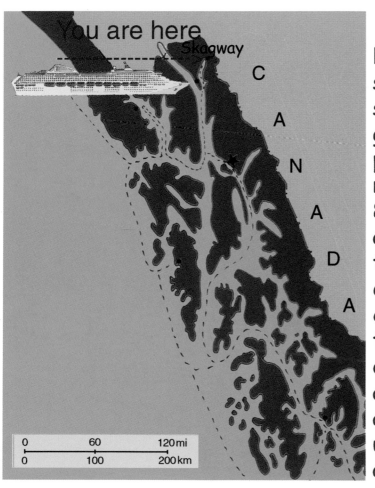

You are here

Skagway

C
A
N
A
D
A

0	60	120 mi
0	100	200 km

Grandma and Grandpa made it back in time to explore the historic sights of the city before their ship sails on. During the height of the gold rushes, more than 20,000 people lived in Skagway. The gold miners are long gone, and only about 800 people live here now year-around. But the frontier houses, the wooden boardwalks, the horse-drawn carriage, and the old-time cars remind us of those exciting times when people came from all over the world in search of gold and adventure. Do you want to be an adventurer when you are grown up? Tell Grandma and Grandpa about your big plans.

This evening is reserved for a very special treat. Grandma and Grandpa are going to the pools! But which one should they choose? Can you believe that there are eight different pools on the ship? Some pools are small and shallow while others are big and deep. One pool even makes waves for swimming against the current like in the ocean. Some pools are filled with cold water, some with warm water, and a few even with steaming hot water. Ask Grandma and Grandpa which one they liked best. Which one would you have picked?

You are ......

here   **or here**   **or here**

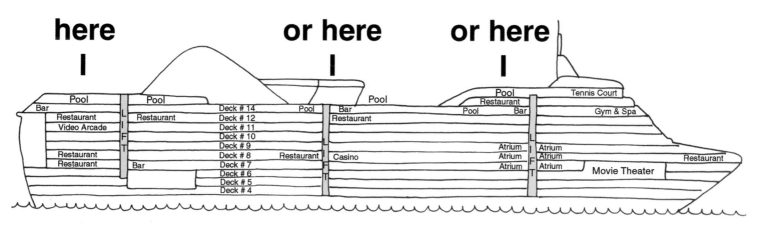

Have you ever seen so many bald eagles all at once? Grandma and Grandpa are stunned! They had heard that this area and the city of Haines in the background are famous for large gatherings of eagles, but they didn't expect anything like this. Can you guess why all these eagles gather here? Grandma and Grandpa learn what attracts the eagles, especially in the winter, are strong salmon runs and the fact that there are hot springs along a nearby river. This lets the eagles catch fish at a time when other rivers are frozen over. I guess even eagles like a hot meal of Alaskan salmon. We told you salmon is yummy!

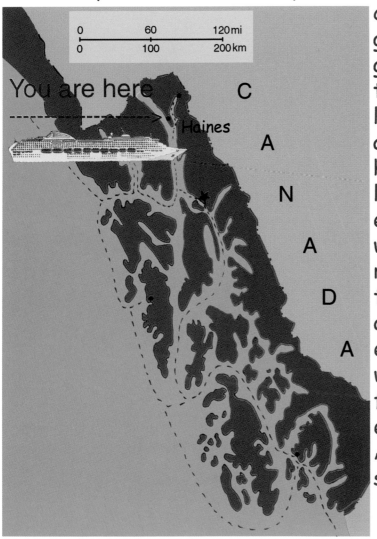

You are here

Haines

C

A

N

A

D

A

0   60   120 mi
0   100   200 km

Last night Grandma and Grandpa cruised to another world-famous area - Glacier Bay. They have come here to see two very special things. First, this is one of the very few places in the world where a record number of glaciers have moved down all the way to the ocean. Such rare glaciers are called tidewater glaciers. What's even more amazing, though, is to watch ice break off from a glacier's face. This is known as 'calving.' KABOOM is the sound it makes when the ice cracks, followed by a big SPLASH as it tumbles into the water. Once in the water, wind and waves take the pieces of ice, sometimes the size of a house or even bigger, and float them away as icebergs.

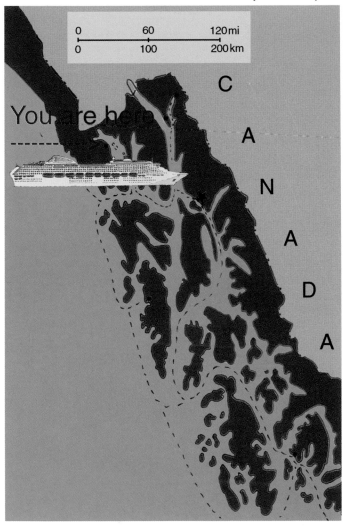

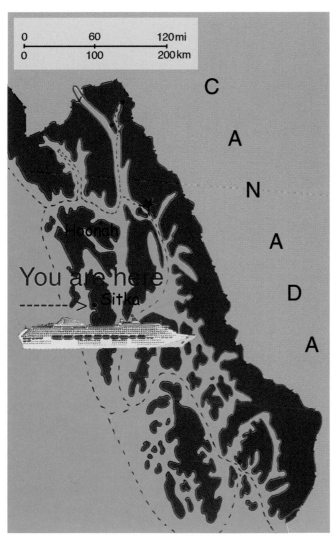

What happened? Did the cruise ship go off course last night and end up in Siberia?

Of course not! We are still in Alaska, in the city of Sitka to be exact. But two hundred years ago Alaska officially belonged to Russia and Sitka was its capital. In 1867 the United States bought Alaska from Russia for $7.2 million and thus made it part of the U.S. territory. Many sites and names in Sitka still remind us of early Russian days. Ask Grandma and Grandpa if their cruise ship went to Sitka or if it went to a different place instead. Maybe it went to Hoonah?

Every vacation has to end at some point and time, and so does this one. As the sun goes down on the last day of the cruise, Grandma and Grandpa remember how much they have seen during the last few days and what a good time they had. They saw some great animals that one usually only sees in a zoo and glaciers that they had known only from TV. They visited some neat historic sites of gold rushes, Native Alaskans, and early Russian fur traders that they had only read about in adventure books. And they experienced all of it from the comfort of a great cruise ship. It was a fantastic trip and they are looking forward to their next cruise. But they are looking forward even more to seeing you!

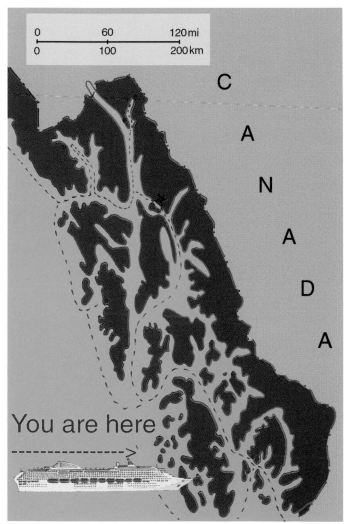

The End.

Your Travel Photos Here

Your Travel Notes Here

Your Travel Photos Here

Your Travel Photos Here

Your Travel Notes Here

More Books and Games by Bernd and Susan Richter

Alaska Children's Books, P.O. Box 872127, Wasilla, AK 99687; www.alaskachildrensbooks.com

She's My Mommy Too!
An Alaskan Tale of Sibling Rivalry

Discover Alaska's Denali Park

DO ALASKANS LIVE IN IGLOOS?

Traveling Alaska

Alaska Animals - Where Do They Go At 40 Below?

Bernd and Susan Richter

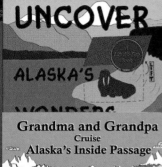

UNCOVER ALASKA'S WONDERS

Grandma and Grandpa Cruise Alaska's Inside Passage

A Children's Book by Bernd and Susan Richter

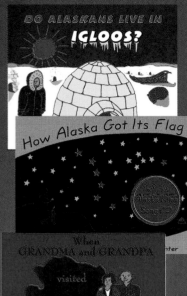

How Alaska Got Its Flag

When GRANDMA visited ALASKA

When GRANDMA and GRANDPA visited ALASKA they ...

A Children's Book by Bernd and Susan Richter

GRANDMA and GRANDPA Visit Denali National Park

by Bernd and Susan Richter
Illustrated by Diane L. Dougherty

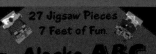

27 Jigsaw Pieces 7 Feet of Fun.

The Alaska ABC Train Puzzle

Puzzles

Alaska Block Puzzle

6 IN 1

12 BLOCKS THAT MAKE
6 DIFFERENT ALASKA PICTURES

Listen to the Alaska Train

by Bernd and Susan Richter

A Bus Ride Into DENALI

Denali National Park and Preserve

Board Books

When Grandma and Grandpa visited Alaska they ...

When Grandma and Grandpa Cruised Through Alaska ...

For all Ages up to 4

When Grandma and Grandpa visited Denali National Park

by Bernd & Susan Richter, Illustrations by Diane L. Dougherty

Card Game

Old Maid

Alaska Style

Good Morning Alaska Good Morning Little Bear

Touch and Feel Alaska's Animals

by Bernd & Susan Richter

Peek-A-Boo Alaska

Goodnight Alaska Goodnight Little Bear

How Animal Moms Love Their Babies

Listen to Alaska's Animals

A Sound Book by Bernd & Susan Richter

and more.

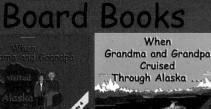

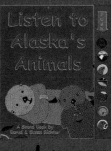